Originally published as *Kleine Beer wil groot worden* in Belgium and Holland
by Clavis Uitgeverij, Hasselt—Amsterdam, 2017
English translation from the Dutch by Clavis Publishing Inc., New York

Visit us on the Web at www.clavis-publishing.com.

Little Bear Wants to Grow written by Judith Koppens and illustrated by Suzanne Diederen

ISBN 978-1-60537-408-6

This book was printed in January 2019 at Wai Man Book Binding (China) Ltd. Flat A, 9/F., Phase 1,
Kwun Tong Industrial Centre, 472-484 Kwun Tong Road, Kwun Tong, Kowloon, H.K.

First Edition
10 9 8 7 6 5 4 3 2 1

Little Bear Wants to GROW

Judith Koppens & Suzanne Diederen

Clavis

NEW YORK

This is Little Bear.
Little Bear would love to grow up.
"Be patient, Little Bear," Mommy and Daddy Bear tell him.
But Little Bear doesn't want to wait.
He decides to ask for help.

Neighbor Bear says:
"Eating ice cream will help you grow."

Little Bear eats so much ice cream,
he becomes a sticky mess.
But Little Bear doesn't grow.

Grandma Bear says:

"You grow from drinking lemonade."

Little Bear drinks at least a hundred glasses of lemonade.
He has to pee a lot.
But Little Bear doesn't grow.

Uncle Bear says:
"Riding your bike makes
you grow."

Little Bear cycles for hours and hours.
It makes him very tired.
But it doesn't make Little Bear grow.

Auntie Bear says:
"You grow from painting."

Little Bear paints all day long.
He is covered in paint.
But Little Bear doesn't grow.

Little Bear is very sad.

"You don't have to do anything to grow," Mommy Bear says to comfort him.
"You grow a little bit every day. Just like that!" says Daddy Bear.

"And a big hug from Mommy and Daddy every day . . . that helps!"
That's how Little Bear grows. A little every day. Just like that.